C0-GBD-521

A dinosaur
that's red,

a dinosaur
that's brown…

WALTER WICK

CAN YOU SEE WHAT I SEE?

DINOSAURS

SCHOLASTIC

Can you see
what I see?

A dinosaur
that's up,

a dinosaur
that's down…

A dinosaur

with plates of blue,

a dinosaur

with flippers, too…

A dinosaur
that's big,

a dinosaur
that's small...

A dinosaur
that's short,

a dinosaur
that's tall...

Which do you like best of all?

Can you say these dinosaur names?

Tyrannosaurus rex

Stegosaurus

Iguanodon

Triceratops

$4.99 US
$6.99 CAN

A dinosaur that's big,
a dinosaur that's small...

Which do you like
best of all?

No part of this publication may be reproduced, stored in a retrieval system, or transmitted in any form or by any means, electronic, mechanical, photocopying, recording, or otherwise, without written permission of the publisher. For information regarding permission, write to Scholastic Inc., Attention: Permissions Department, 557 Broadway, New York, NY 10012.

Copyright © 2006 by Walter Wick.
All rights reserved. Published by Scholastic Inc.
SCHOLASTIC, CARTWHEEL BOOKS, and associated logos
are trademarks and/or registered trademarks of Scholastic Inc.

Images on pages 5, 7, 9, 11, 13, and 14/15 taken from *Can You See What I See? Cool Collections*
© 2004 by Walter Wick. Published by Scholastic Inc.

ISBN 0-439-83297-7

10 9 8 7 6 5 4 3 2 1 06 07 08 09 10

Printed in China • First printing, May 2006

Cartwheel BOOKS

an imprint of
SCHOLASTIC
www.scholastic.com

ISBN 0-439-83297-7
EAN
9 780439 832977
50499